Eric Carle

The Very Busy Spider

aaron

Scholastic Books Inc.
New York

Early one morning the wind blew a spider across the field.
A thin, silky thread trailed from her body.
The spider landed on a fence post near a farm yard . . .

and began to spin a web with her silky thread.

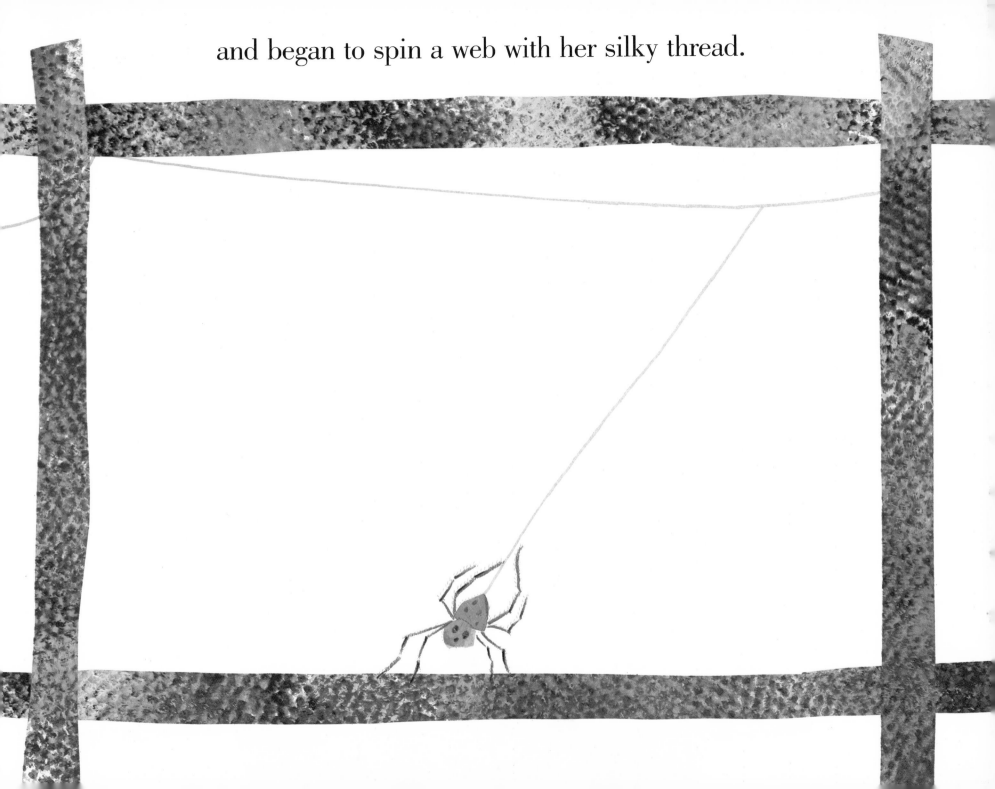

"Neigh! Neigh!" said the horse. "Want to go for a ride?"

The spider didn't answer. She was very busy spinning her web.

"Moo! Moo!" said the cow. "Want to eat some grass?"

The spider didn't answer. She was very busy spinning her web.

"Baa! Baa!" bleated the sheep. "Want to run in the meadow?"

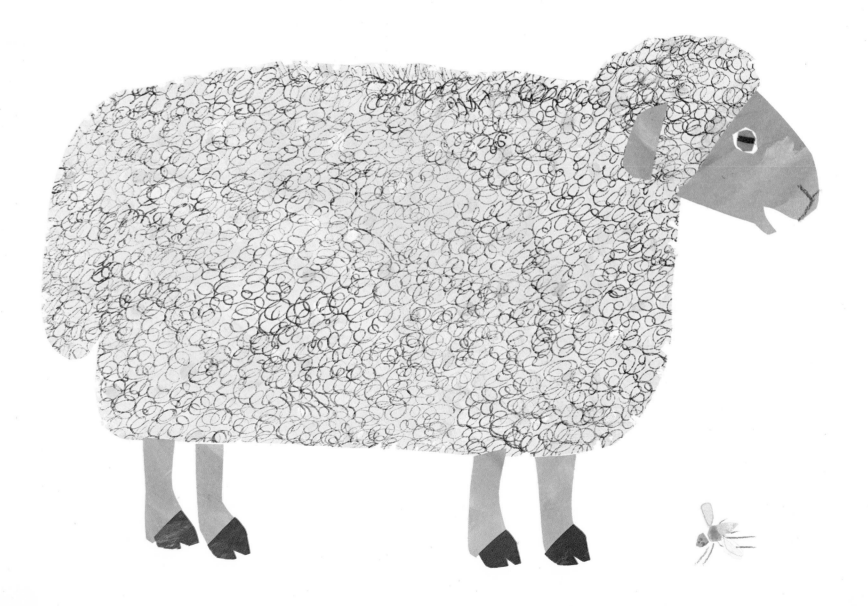

The spider didn't answer. She was very busy spinning her web.

"Maa! Maa!" said the goat. "Want to jump on the rocks?"

The spider didn't answer. She was very busy spinning her web.

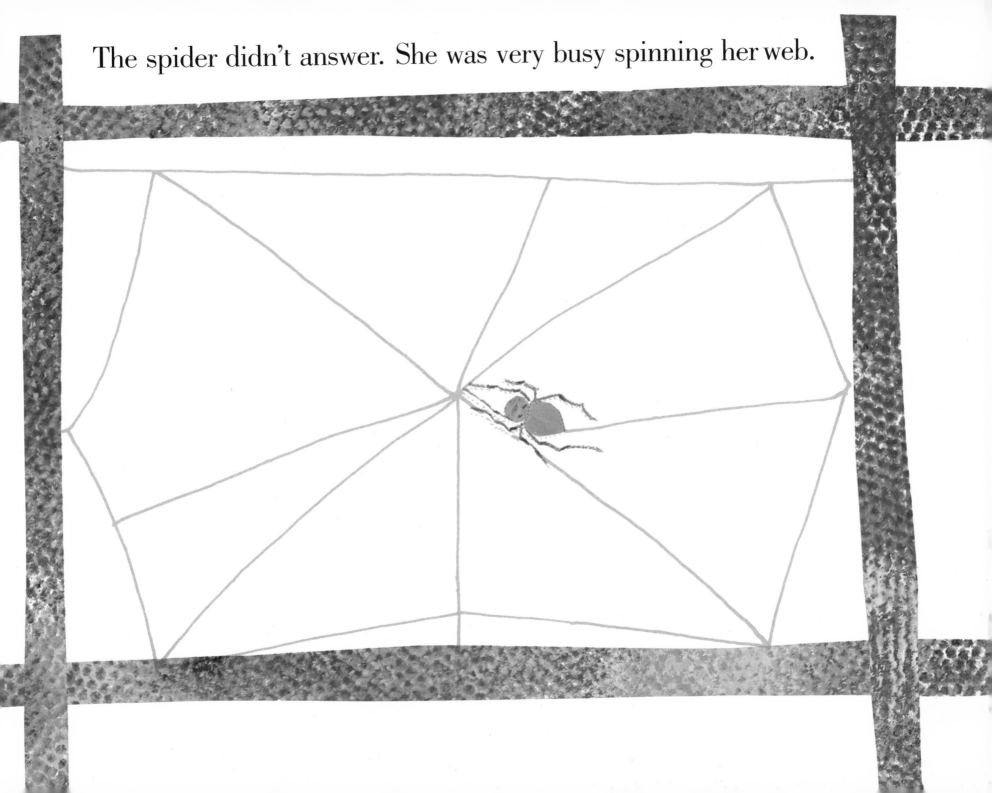

"Oink! Oink!" grunted the pig. "Want to roll in the mud?"

The spider didn't answer. She was very busy spinning her web.

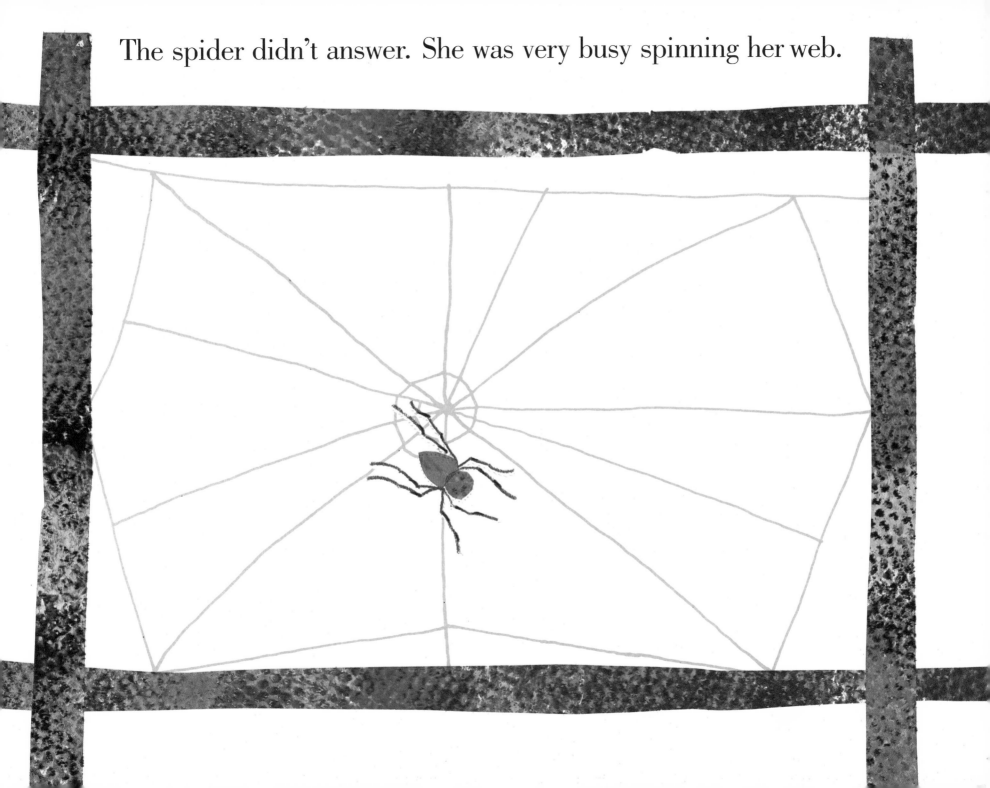

"Woof! Woof!" barked the dog. "Want to chase a cat?"

The spider didn't answer. She was very busy spinning her web.

"Meow! Meow!" cried the cat. "Want to take a nap?"

The spider didn't answer. She was very busy spinning her web.

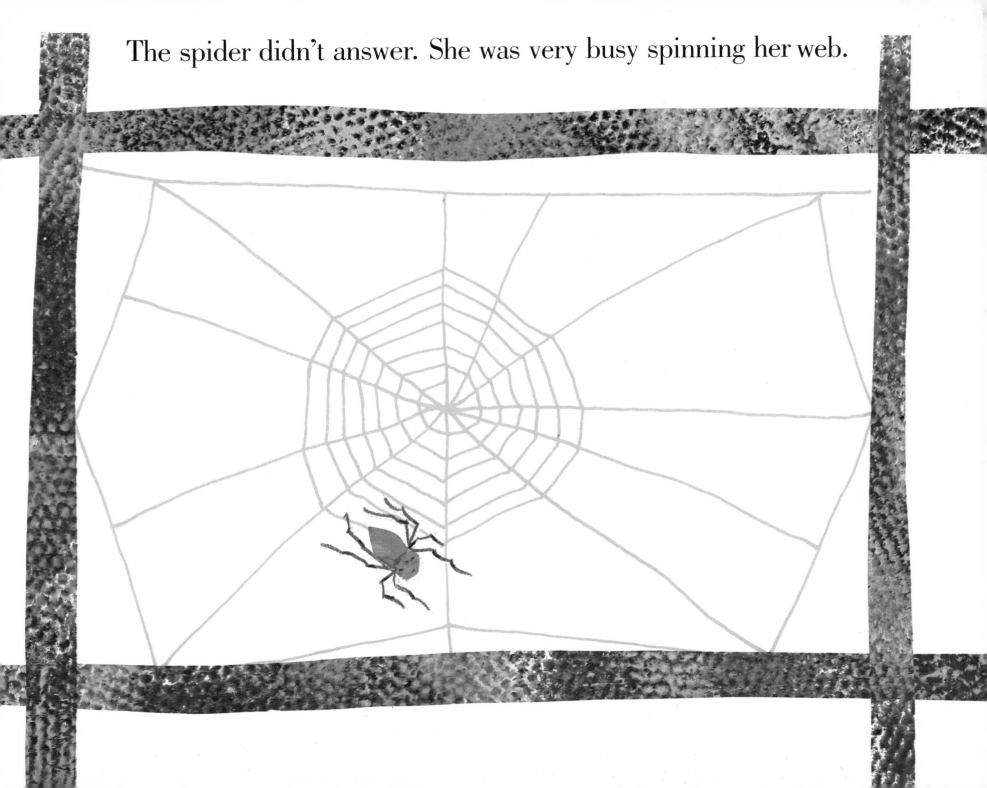

"Quack! Quack!" called the duck. "Want to go for a swim?"

And th The spider didn't answer. She had now finished her web.

"Coc

"Whoo? Whoo?"
asked the owl.
"Who built this
beautiful web?"
The spider
didn't answer.
She had
fallen asleep.

It had been
a very, very
busy day.